# Planet Cake

Written by **Teresa Heapy**

Illustrated by **Ana García**

**OXFORD**
UNIVERSITY PRESS

# OXFORD
## UNIVERSITY PRESS

Great Clarendon Street, Oxford, OX2 6DP, United Kingdom

Oxford University Press is a department of the University
of Oxford. It furthers the University's objective of excellence
in research, scholarship, and education by publishing
worldwide. Oxford is a registered trade mark of Oxford
University Press in the UK and in certain other countries

British Library Cataloguing in Publication Data
Data available

ISBN: 978-0-19-841506-0

10 9 8 7 6 5 4 3 2 1

Paper used in the production of this book is a natural, recyclable product
made from wood grown in sustainable forests. The manufacturing process
conforms to the environmental regulations of the country of origin.

Printed in China by Golden Cup

**Acknowledgements**

Series Editor: Nikki Gamble

Beth had a rocket.

"I am going to visit a different planet!" she said.

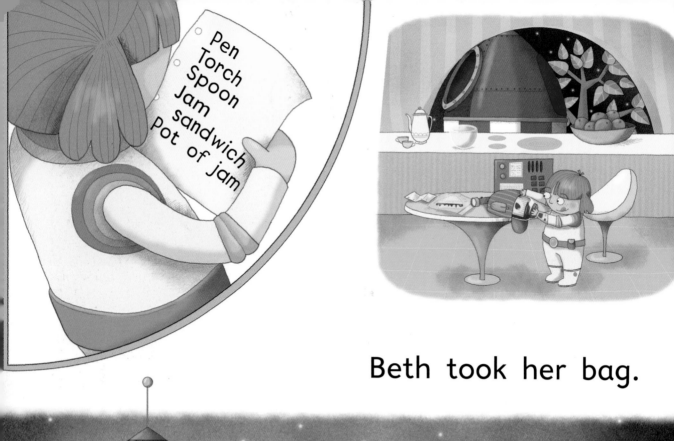

Pen
Torch
Spoon
Jam sandwich
Pot of jam

Beth took her bag.

She put on her helmet.
She got into her rocket.

The rocket shot
into the sky.

It landed
on a planet.

THUMP!

Beth got out.

"There are just rocks on this planet," she said.

"Not just rocks," said a Cake-bot.
"They are rock *cakes*."

"Hmm," said Beth. "This cake
is a bit dry."

"*What?*" said the Cake-bot.

"I think this cake needs some ... **jam**!" said Beth.

Beth split the rock cake.
She put some jam on it.

"**Mmmm!**" said the Cake-bot.
"It's good!"

Beth and the Cake-bot put jam on lots of cakes.

"That is a **big** cake!" said Beth.

"Thank you," said
the Cake-bot.

Beth got back into her rocket.

Beth was back
on her planet.

"I can see Planet Cake!"
she said.